Ding Dong

by Geoff Smith & Katie C. Stan

Illustrated by Ron Zalme

SCHOLASTIC INC.

New York   Toronto   London   Auckland   Sydney
Mexico City   New Delhi   Hong Kong   Buenos Aires

Published by Scholastic Inc.,
90 Old Sherman Turnpike, Danbury, Connecticut 06816.

SCHOLASTIC and associated logos are trademarks
and/or registered trademarks of Scholastic Inc.

ISBN 0-439-56276-7

First Scholastic Printing, December 2003

Chapters

Chapter 1
Summer Bored, Some Are Not

It was a hot summer day, and Timmy Turner was sweaty and bored.

"How about we go to the movies?" his father suggested.

"Soda, popcorn, and air-conditioning,"
Timmy sighed happily. "That sounds great!"

"It sure does!" said Mr. Turner. "But I
meant your mother and me—*not* you."

"Besides, we know how much fun you
always have with Vicky," said Mrs. Turner.
"We'll be back at six o' clock. Buh-bye!"

As soon as Mr. and Mrs. Turner were out

of earshot, Timmy's archenemy baby-sitter commanded, "I want to be alone—to your room, Twerp!"

Timmy sighed and trudged upstairs to his room.

Chapter 2
Winter Games

"Summer is so boring!" Timmy complained to his fairy godparents, Cosmo and Wanda. "I wish it weren't so hot!"

"Oooh, let's make some
winter!" suggested Cosmo.

Wanda agreed. "That would cool things
off and maybe even cheer you up, Kiddo."

POOF!

Timmy's closet suddenly became a giant
ice rink. A light snow was falling.

Timmy cheered, rushed over to the door
to his room, and locked each of the locks.
"There. That should keep Vicky out,"
he said. "Now, let's play some hockey!"

A moment later the game was on. "Hit me with your best shot!" called Wanda from her position in front of the goal.

"Wheee! Hockey is fun . . . in a painful

kind of way," added Cosmo the Hockey

Puck as he whizzed through the air.

Chapter 3
Snow Problem

Awhile later, Cosmo and Wanda were feeling anything but hot. Wanda let out a huge sneeze. "I'b going to sit down, Tibby," she said stuffily. "I'b not feeling—a-a-ahhh-choo!—very well."

"Me, too. I have a headache," said Cosmo.
"For some reason, I keep hearing
bells ringing."

"Uh-oh, Cosbo. You've taken too bany
slap shots to the head," worried Wanda.

Just then Timmy heard footsteps and jingling keys.

"I hear fun in there," warned Vicky, "AND IT'S GOTTA STOP!"

Timmy looked at his fairy godparents with alarm and ran to the door. "Oh no! Quick, guys! I wish that Vicky hadn't found my keys."

"Did you hear what Tibby said?" Wanda asked Cosmo. "By head is all stuffy, and by ears are all plugged."

"Mostly I heard *dingdong, dingdong,*" complained Cosmo. "But I'm pretty sure Timmy said he wanted monkeys."

"*Bonkeys?!?*" Wanda repeated in disbelief.

"Why would Tibby want bonkeys? Well, his
wish is our command, after all—" Cosmo
and Wanda waved their wands.

Suddenly four monkeys appeared.

As Timmy gaped at his new guests, the door slammed open. "What are those monkeys doing in here?" Vicky demanded.

"Making a mess?" Timmy replied uncertainly.

"You are *so* busted!" Vicky shrieked. At the sound of her voice, all four monkeys looked up and shrieked in response.

Vicky backed away as the monkeys moved toward her. They moved closer and closer. At the last minute, Vicky made a dash for the open doorway and took off running down the hall. The four monkeys followed close behind, chattering happily to each other.

Chapter 4
Monkey Roundup

Timmy, Cosmo, and Wanda tore after
the monkeys. By the time they reached the
kitchen, Vicky and her monkey mob had
disappeared out the front door.

"What are we going to do?" Timmy
shouted.

Cosmo struggled to catch his breath.
"Wanda and I are in no shape to chase after
monkeys," he panted. "And I wish someone
would answer that phone!"

"Tibby, if you'll round up the
bonkeys and bring theb back to us, we can
take care of the rest," Wanda offered.

"I . . . well . . . ," Timmy said
hesitantly, then replied, "of course!"

POOF!

"No! I didn't say *horse!* I said . . . oh, never mind," sighed Timmy, jumping into the saddle.

NEIGH

Timmy quickly rounded up three of the monkeys and headed back to the house.

"Hey, Timmy, nice horse and monkeys! Where'd you get them?" asked his friend Chester, as Timmy galloped by.

"Err . . . the Internet," replied Timmy
over his shoulder. "Everything's just a
click away."

When Timmy returned with
the monkeys, Wanda waved her
wand and said, "There you go,
little guys, back to where you
cabe frob."

"Hey, Timmy, don't you still have another monkey to catch?" Cosmo asked.

Timmy looked around desperately. Out in the yard, he saw Vicky climbing a tree. The last monkey was closing in on her.

Wanda followed Timmy's gaze. "Oh, by," she sniffled. "It looks like that bonkey has grown rather fond of Vicky!"

"Get away from me, you ugly ape!" Vicky was screeching. "When I get my hands on that twerp, Timmy . . . "

"Oh no!" groaned Timmy, trying not to panic. "Cosmo, Wanda—listen carefully: I wish you'd make that monkey go!"

"Make the monkey *grow?*" repeated Cosmo and Wanda at the same time.

Instantly the monkey became enormous. He grabbed Vicky in one hand and then began climbing up the side of Timmy's house.

Timmy smacked his forehead. "Oh, man!
I wish I'd just kept my mouth closed!"
he muttered.

"You say, you wish we'd made your *house
grow?*" Cosmo asked, confused. "I don't see

how that's going to help, but whatever you say, Timmy!"

Swooosh! Timmy's house shot up into the sky.

"Cosmo, why would I wish for such a giant house?" shouted Timmy at the top of his lungs.

Cosmo shrugged. "Well, everyone can use more closet space."

Timmy looked at his watch. "My parents will be home in 10 minutes! I'd better think of something fast!" he gasped.

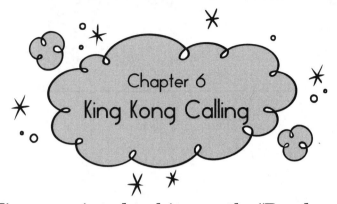

Chapter 6
King Kong Calling

Timmy pointed to his mouth. "Read my lips!" he told Cosmo and Wanda in his loudest, clearest voice. "I wish I had a HE-LI-COP-TER." He made a whirling gesture with both hands.

"You said *helicopter,* right?" asked Wanda.

"Yes!" Timmy shouted.

"Well, that's the first sensible thing you've wished for all day," Cosmo said.

POOF!

Timmy jumped into the helicopter and flew up to save Vicky.

"Vicky, jump on!" Timmy shouted.

"No way, Runt!" she screamed back. "You don't even have a driver's license!"

Vicky turned her attention back to the love-struck monkey. "Take your stinking paws off me, you smelly ape!" she shouted. With a hurt look, the giant monkey set Vicky down on the roof and backed away.

INTERRUPT!

"I'd like to take this bobent to point out to our readers that bonkeys are not apes," Wanda explained. "While bonkeys and apes are both anthropoid pribates, it would be incorrect—"

"And I'd like to point out that someone still needs to answer that ringing phone!" interrupted Cosmo.

"Oh, dear," said Wanda, blowing her nose. "I was hoping your ringing ears would have cleared up by now."

MONKEY

Meanwhile up on the roof, the giant monkey was trying to get away from the wrath of Vicky. The poor, frightened creature reached out and grabbed onto the helicopter to escape.

Timmy set the monkey on the ground next to Wanda and then landed the helicopter.

Cosmo returned the house to its normal size and a very confused Vicky climbed down from the roof just as Timmy's parents arrived home.

"Hi, Son," Timmy's father greeted him cheerfully. "Looks like you, Vicky, and your giant ape had fun in your helicopter today!"

"Maybe I'm lucky my parents are clueless," Timmy confided to the monkey.

Chapter 7
Seems Like
Cold Times

Later that evening, everything was back
to normal.

"From now on, when I have a boring day," Timmy said, "I'll leave it that way!"

"Look what I found!" Cosmo held up a puck. "How about we use this thing the next time we play hockey?" he suggested.

Timmy and his fairy godparents headed down the hall to his room.

"Wait!" cried Wanda. "We forgot . . . DON'T open your—"

But it was too late.

Timmy turned the knob, and . . .

. . . *THUMP*. A huge pile of snow fell on Timmy's head.

"Sorry about the snow!" Wanda clucked. "Want a tissue?"

"*Kiss* you?" Timmy asked. "I'd better not. I think I just caught a cold."

CHOO!